Beyond the

Tempest Gate

Beyond the
Tempest Gate

By Jeff Suwak

Vabella Publishing
P.O. Box 1052
Carrollton, GA 30112
www.vabella.com

First Edition: August 2013

Printed in the United States of America

Cover Designer: Tamian Wood, BeyondDesignInternational.com

Cover sword image courtesy of Calimacil, www.calimacil.com

This is a work of fiction. Names, characters, places and incidents are either the product of the author's imagination or are used fictitiously, and any resemblance to actual persons living or dead, events, or locales is entirely fictitious.

ISBN 978-1-938230-44-8

Library of Congress Control Number 2013912340

10 9 8 7 6 5 4 3 2 1

To Kim.

Thank you.

ACKNOWLEDGMENTS

Jeremiah Thek offered invaluable creative input during the early stages of writing this book.

T.L. Gray taught me more than I can ever repay about the business of writing, and reminded me to laugh whenever I started to let the work consume me.

Alexis A. Hunter was always on call to give feedback during the thousand or so revisions that went into this book.

Christian Fennell reminded me what's really important.

PART ONE

The Tempest Gate was visible on the horizon long before Gabriel sailed into it – a black vortex of roiling clouds, pulsing and veined with lightning, churning over the sea like newly erupted volcanic ash. For five hundred years sailors had been changing course at the very sight of that unholy deluge, but Gabriel, Holy Knight of the Church of Dunrabian, headed straight for its very heart. He had come to destroy the demon Elezear sleeping within its elemental walls, and he would complete his quest or die trying.

The roar of the Gate enveloped him as he drew near. Sheets of rain cascaded from the sky and pounded into the sea with a thunderous din like thousands of warhorses charging over a battlefield. The sound rattled his teeth and sent a bolt of panic running through his spine. Biting down hard against his fear, the young man held steady to his course.

He had no right to cowardice. His mission was to rid the world of the evil that was Elezear, and that task was more important than his own life. Victory over the demon would require absolute conviction. There was no room for hesitation or doubt. Sneering with disdain at both the Gate and his own weakness, he trimmed his ship's lone sail and sped headlong into the wall of storm.

The first winds splintered his mast and sent the sail fluttering into the water like a ruined kite. Stinging rain lashed

1

across his face like needles. Darkness enveloped him so completely it was as if he had been struck blind, able to make out the raging, insane seascape around him only in periodic flashes and bursts of lightning. Waves crashed and exploded against each other, splitting the air with the blasts of their impact. Gabriel picked up the oars from the hull of the boat and rowed.

Whipped back and forth, spun around and several times nearly capsized, the knight quickly lost sense of what direction he was headed in. He was simply fighting to stay afloat, balancing the little vessel against the ocean's malevolent will.

Gabriel laughed. All of his twenty-five years of life had been building towards that moment. Countless hours of training, sacrifice, and prayer had all been spent in preparation for the battle that lie ahead. He shouted at the sky, "It will take more than a warm breeze and some mist to turn me back."

As if in response to his impudence, the winds raged harder, the rain turned to hail, and a towering form rose in the distance, its silhouette impressed upon the curtains of precipitation in a lightning burst of illumination. Gabriel at first thought a mountain had come within view, but then the lightning cracked again and revealed the black shape in its entirety. It was no mountain. It was a wave, and it was moving his way. The knight pulled the oars inside the boat, gripped the sides, and held on.

The impact smashed the ship to splinters and sent him flying into the ocean. He recovered from the shock to find himself sinking like a stone into the soundless, underwater darkness, his body growing numb and unresponsive in the frigid cold. Unable to discern direction in the lightless depths, he swam against the sinking feeling, hoping he moved upwards.

He kicked off his boots and shed his tunic to rid himself of their weight. The sword sheathed in his belt was heaviest of all, of course, but he would drown before he gave that up, and if it became lost, he would die chasing it into the depths. It was the Sword of Dunrabian, and he was nothing if not its Arm.

The breath he'd taken was quickly used up. His diaphragm strained and heaved. Hypoxia lights floated before his eyes as he clawed at the water like a falling climber grasping for a handhold, lungs ready to explode as he fought his body's reflexive attempts to take a fatal breath of air that was not there. Gagging on nothing. Mind fuzzy and spinning. He did not know if he was moving closer to the surface or farther away, but there was no other choice.

Don't let me fail now, Dunrabian, he prayed. *Not when I'm so close to fulfilling the purpose you created me for.*

It seemed that his prayer would go unanswered and he would drown alone in the frigid darkness, but just before he lost control of his lungs, he broke through the ocean's surface. It took three full breaths to clear his mind enough to grasp the fact that he was no longer submerged. His relief was fleeting, for he quickly realized that his situation wasn't much improved. Waves pummeled him on every side. Torrents of rain splashed off the ocean's roiling surface so that he choked on water every time he breathed. His muscles were fatiguing, and the numbness created by the cold continued to spread. He could not swim forever.

A flash of lightning illuminated something bobbing in the water. Lunging for the object, Gabriel thrashed about in the darkness trying to find it. To his amazement, he found himself grasping hold of a section of his ship's shattered mast-pole. Clutching the spar close to his chest, he rested his head upon it. "Thank you, Dunrabian," he whispered. "Thank you."

Floating atop his makeshift raft, the knight scanned the horizon for some indication of the direction he needed to head towards. There was no room for error in the next move he made. His energy was almost entirely spent. Exhaustion and cold would soon overtake him. If he made a mistake, there would not be an opportunity for another.

A glimpse of light appeared in the distance. It was there only for a moment, and then disappeared just as quickly behind the rollicking waves. It was gone so fast that Gabriel was not certain he had seen it at all, but with no other choices left to him, he headed in the direction of the illumination.

He did not know how long he swam. There was no sun to mark time, and no landscape features to gauge distance. He only knew that after what felt like a very, very long time, he still had not located either light or land. His legs began to fail him. He willed them into motion, but they did not move him far. Eventually, they did not move him at all. Pedaling uselessly in place while waves tossed him about like driftwood, Gabriel howled in defiance.

He did not fear death. He only feared failure in his quest. If he had to die, he prayed that it was not there in the water, but in battle with Elezear.

The ocean swelled beneath him. A wave swept him up and sent him surging through the hail, rain, and darkness. It grew higher and higher as it went, towering over the sea. At the moment of the wave's apex, Gabriel saw light in the distance again. It seemed closer than before, though how close, he could not be sure. The wave broke. Holding the spar close to him, the knight prepared for impact.

The force of the crashing wave sent him shooting and spinning into the cold depths. He reached out to catch the spar as it was ripped from his arms, but was not quick enough. As he watched the wood disappear into the nebulous deep, it occurred to him that he could see again.

He stopped swimming and looked about in mute wonder. No longer cast in darkness, a faint light now permeated the water all around him. Not the flashing radiance of lightning, but instead a persistent glow. He searched around for the source of the light when a powerful current caught him, twisted him about, and smashed his head against something hard. There was a crunching sound, a brilliant explosion of pain, and then he fell into a different kind of darkness altogether.

Jeff Suwak

PART TWO

Only weeks earlier, Nimphus had tried to talk Gabriel out of challenging the demon. The aged priest never came out and ordered him to remain at home, but Gabriel could see the doubt and the fear in the old man's eyes as he sat facing him across an ivory table within the windowless Prayer Room. As always, hundreds of white candles burned along the walls of the voluminous chamber. On any other night, an attendant would have walked up and down those rows, replacing each light before it had a chance to burn out. But, on that night, there was no such servant. There was only Gabriel, Nimphus, and the battle being fought in the unspoken words between them.

"I hear you've begun preparations for your journey across the sea," Nimphus said, attempting a wan smile on his thin, pale lips.

"I've only ordered the building of a boat, Esteemed Father," Gabriel answered, feigning nervousness at a possible rebuke, "in interest of being ready for when the time comes to depart. I would not begin the outfitting of my journey until I had your consent."

Nimphus laughed. That mirth, at least, seemed authentic. The old man always did adore deference and humility. "I am accusing you of no ill intent, my son. I am merely asking you about the news I hear. It's a hard habit to break, you know, after so many years of rescuing you from your own courage."

Now it was Gabriel's turn to fumble with an awkward grin. "I certainly have had the easier half of our relationship, Esteemed Father."

"Yes," Nimphus said. "But I've had the happier half. It's always more enjoyable to watch a boy grow into a man, than to watch a man decay into a fossil." The priest laughed, but his eyes looked sad and wistful.

Gabriel's fake chuckle tripped over itself and fell flat, leaving the room in an awkward silence. He hated the tension that had grown between them. Nimphus was the High Ecclesiastic, head of the Church of Dunrabian, which made him the most powerful man in the Five Kingdoms. More importantly than that lofty position, Nimphus was like Gabriel's second father. The man had nurtured, encouraged, and mentored the knight for twelve years of his life. Gabriel had taken a sacred vow to die in his service, if necessary, and he had meant every word that he said. Yet, on that evening, he found himself restraining anger at his benefactor while they played a deceitful game of politics.

"I wish we could sit and talk for hours as we used to," Nimphus said, signaling that the time had come to end their pleasantries and get to the real business at hand. "I wish I could hear about all the things that you were learning from your tutors, and all the skills that you were picking up from the warrior monks. But, as you know, Church business must always take precedence over family." He studied Gabriel for a long moment. "Especially in a matter as grave as the one you bring before me."

The use of the word *family* was no accident, Gabriel knew. It was an attempt to win over his sentimentality. He was fully aware this, but took no more offense to the emotional ploy than he would take to a punch thrown in a game of fists. For all the honest affection between the two men, they each had a role to play in this game, and both intended to win.

The biggest advantage that the knight had was the fact that Nimphus very likely imagined that his opponent was oblivious to their contest. It was not that the priest ever accused him of being dimwitted throughout their years together, but he often teased him for his hardheadedness and lack of intellectual finesse. The old man still saw the boy that Gabriel used to be, and could not possibly have known all the noncombat skills he had been picking up while traveling in foreign lands, and taking lessons on the nuances of diplomacy. His studies had led him into some rather loathful company, for sure, but it was his duty to do anything and everything necessary to ensure the completion of his mission. He had foreseen that night's conversation in the Prayer Room long before it ever happened, and had been preparing for it.

"What matter do you wish to discuss, Esteemed Father?" Gabriel struggled to keep his tone conversational, as though oblivious to the real matter at hand, a naïf caught up in matters beyond the limitations of his temperament. Direct confrontation with the High Ecclesiastic would go badly, and a more circuitous strategy was called for. "Do you have any ideas you'd like to share for my journey to the Tempest Gate?"

"I have not approved that journey yet," Nimphus said, his tone becoming more firm and authoritative. "Have you not already said as much yourself?"

"Of course," Gabriel nodded, understanding that they were now fully embroiled in the negotiation. "I simply imagined that it was a foregone conclusion, and that approval was but a formality."

"What would make you think such a thing?"

Gabriel paused for a moment before answering, forcing a quizzical expression onto his face. "Well, the fact that my mission was ordered by Dunrabian, Esteemed Father."

Nimphus squinted. Suspicion lighted in his eyes for a moment, as though wondering for the first time just how much his adopted son had matured in the years they'd grown apart.

"Of course," the High Ecclesiastic said, careful not to sound as though he might doubt a divinely issued command. "We must always honor Dunrabian's will." He leaned his head back and stared up at the ceiling, nodding to himself as though in deep contemplation. It was a technique Gabriel had seen him use many times before, in order to buy himself time to prepare the proper response to an unexpected statement. No one dared interrupt the High Ecclesiastic in the midst of thinking.

Gabriel had intentionally used a religious decree to put Nimphus on the defensive, and it had worked, but he felt no pride in the success of his subterfuge. He would not have undertaken the conversation in the first place if it was not absolutely necessary to his mission. As unpleasant as the exchange was bound to become, it was essential to his plans.

If Gabriel had been anyone other than the Holy Knight, he knew, Nimphus would have denied his request without a moment's hesitation. It was not the pair's close, personal bond that made a difference. No, the only thing that complicated the priest's refusal was the fact that Gabriel's reputation had grown to such great proportions that not even the High Ecclesiastic could lightly dismiss it.

At only twenty-five years old, he had already led the Church's armies to victory over the heathen tribes of the south. He had challenged the pagan giant Emir, and left him dead in the snows atop his mountain. He had hunted down every last dragon in the civilized lands, rooted them out of their dens, and snuffed them out completely. He was hero to royalty and commoners alike. A single utterance from his mouth would divide the Church's armies in half, drawing tens of thousands of men to his side, eager to fight and die in his name. Nimphus was the High Ecclesiastic, but in the eyes of the soldiers, that position garnered little more respect than an aristocrat's would. Gabriel was a warrior and a knight. More than these things, he was the very Arm of the Sword of Dunrabian. He'd earned the soldier's respect in the manner that they respected most – with blood, sweat, and courage on the battlefield.

Seemingly unable to come up with an appropriate riposte, Nimphus sighed and pinched the bridge of his nose wearily. "The Tempest Gate has guarded us from Elezear for five hundred years," he said. "The demon has not afflicted us in all that time. Why disturb it now? Why tempt that battle?"

Despite his advanced years, the willowy High Ecclesiastic normally possessed a boyish energy and enthusiasm that made him seem untouched by time. But in that moment, he looked every bit his age, if not many winters older. With his drooping face, dark circles around his bloodshot eyes, and his back hunched over as though broken beneath a heavy burden, he looked like nothing more than an exhausted relic.

Gabriel looked steadily into Nimpus' eyes. "I must destroy the demon, Esteemed Father, because that is the task that our god appointed to me. It was commanded in the Vision. It's the whole reason I was made for this world."

Nimphus sighed. He looked down at the ivory table before him, absently stroking the topaz ring on his finger as though polishing it. The nervous habit was something that Gabriel had witnessed many times, and long despised for the lack of discipline it revealed. This time, the knight was glad to see the compulsive motion. It meant that Nimphus recognized the trap he was in – the trap that Gabriel had planned on exploiting long before he actually stepped into that room. Not even the High Ecclesiastic of the Church of Dunrabian could argue against the law of the Vision.

Hundreds of years before, the Seers of the Book prophesied that a boy would be born who would one day become the Holy Knight. He would lead the Church to new glory, and be blessed with the power to destroy Elezear. This boy would be visited by a vision sent directly from Dunrabian, and would thereby be marked as the one selected to be lead the Church's army.

The details of that Vision were concealed from the public, passed down in utmost secrecy amongst the highest ranks of the Church, waiting for the day when the child would appear that would describe it in perfect detail. No one outside of a small, select circle knew the contents of the epiphany, which meant that only the authentic, chosen boy could recite it.

Gabriel, born of peasant stock, was the one that emerged from the fields and stunned the Church with his story. He recited every detail in perfect clarity. Nimphus himself verified the recounting of the Vision, though his face had been filled with hesitation throughout the ordeal. Later, he was also the one to knight Gabriel and place the Church's armies under his leadership.

"Only now," Nimphus muttered into the air, caressing the ring, "as the actual undertaking of this quest draws near, does the grave reality of its implications strike me." He looked at Gabriel through sallow eyes. "You petition me to bless an action that could very well mean the destruction of the world. How am I to make such a decision?"

Gabriel gripped his hands into fists and hid them under the ivory table. The subtleties and sleights of diplomatic conversation were distasteful to his nature and roused an instinctive disgust. Everything within him said to pick up his sword and go, to charge headlong into the Tempest Gate, but this situation demanded more restraint. Even knowing this, and despite all his preparations, he ultimately failed in concealing his temper and hammered a fist down on the table. "You should make this decision the same way that you make any decision, Esteemed Father. With faith."

Nimphus looked startled for a moment, eyes growing wide at the experience of being spoken to in such an authoritative tone. He opened his mouth as though to reprimand the young knight, but only sighed and shook his head before slumping further into his seat.

Gabriel saw the fear in Nimphus' eyes, and simultaneously hated and pitied him for it. A fierce love for the man still burned in his heart, but the calling of his destiny flamed brighter. For Nimphus, the Book always came second to the Church. His secular duties always outweighed his sacred ones. Gabriel could not allow the conflict in the old man's heart to delay his quest to destroy the demon.

As much as Gabriel loved the man, the fact was that Nimphus lacked the unbending resolve of a true disciple. The priest wished to deny Gabriel his quest because he lacked perfect faith that the Holy Knight would prevail. If it were not for the fact that Nimphus was equally afraid of the ramifications of denying Gabriel, he already would have refused him, but such a denial would threaten the credibility of his own position as High Ecclesiastic. It could erode the very foundations of the position.

For Nimphus to deny the divine mission of the Holy Knight that he himself had ordained would be to deny the validity of the Vision. To deny the validity of the Vision would be to deny the Book which prophesied the Vision, which would then be a denial of the very source from which Nimphus drew his authority in the first place. Refusing Gabriel's quest would be refusing his own Church, and subsequently, his own position as its leader. It was a paradox that Gabriel already anticipated, and planned to use long before he ever stepped foot in that room.

As if coming to terms with his powerlessness, Nimphus straightened in his chair and ceased the nervous massaging of his ring. "Of course you must go," he said, trying to fill his voice with a stern resolve that clearly was not really there. "It is Dunrabian's will."

The old man hesitated a moment, squinting into the air as

though searching for something to add. "First, you must take three days of meditation on this matter. It has been many years since you had the Vision, Gabriel. You were only a boy. Make certain that Elezear's destruction is still what Dunrabian wants of you."

He fixed Gabriel with a sincere, almost pleading gaze, as though begging the knight to release him from the game he was being forced to play. "There is still so much work for you to do here, Gabriel. Important work. The Church is reaching new heights, and I want you to be at the helm while we rise."

"I will take those reigns of my duty, as always, with the utmost honor and humility," Gabriel said, "after I have destroyed Elezear." He got up from his chair and knelt before the High Ecclesiastic. "Thank you for your blessing, Esteemed Father."

Nimphus sighed, probably disappointed that his final entreaty to Gabriel's restraint had failed. "Meditate for three days," he said, a slight quavering audible in his voice, as though the words were barely holding back more forceful, or fearful, ones. "Think all the good you can do here, at home."

"As you command, Esteemed Father." Gabriel stood and backed out of the chamber.

On his way back to his room, he laughed at the High Ecclesiastic's words. He would take three days of meditation, as commanded, but there would be no deliberation. He'd made his decision long ago, and nothing could sway him from it. Nimphus lacked enough conviction to gamble the lives of the world against the glory of their god, but Gabriel did not suffer from such weakness or doubt. He had all the faith he needed for such a quest. All that, and much more.

PART THREE

Gabriel opened his eyes to find himself lying upon a black-sanded beach beneath a blue and cloudless sky. Confused to find himself shirtless and barefooted, it took him a moment to recall shedding his clothes during his fight for survival in the water. His hand shot reflexively to his sword, and he sighed with relief to find it still sheathed in his belt. Gripping the handle hard to reassure himself with its presence, he sat up facing the sea.

The Tempest Gate loomed less than a quarter-mile offshore. Gabriel watched the ring of storm clouds, the roiling sea, and the blackened wall of mist and rain between them that gave the wall its name. Only by the glory of Dunrabian could he have survived that journey, he decided. Before he could get to his knees for prayer, something moved in the sands behind him. He shot to his feet and turned in a fighting position.

A black-scaled reptile crouched motionless a few feet away, frozen in mid-stride. It was longer than Gabriel was tall. Knife-like claws dangled from its feet and a mottled spattering of red covered its face as though stained with blood. Not a muscle of the beast moved but for the tongue slithering in and out of its mouth, forked end lapping at the air. Dozens more of the things waited in the distant sands, watching the stand-off play out.

The knight drew his sword, dug his feet into the sand for traction, and relaxed his shoulders. His thick, black hair hung in

15

his eyes. Holding his blade aloft with one hand, he swept the hair away with the other. It tore from his head painfully with a ripping sound, reopening the gash that had coagulated there. A warm wave of fresh blood ran over his face.

The monster tensed at the scent. Its tongue quickened. Gabriel wiped the blood from his face and flicked it to the ground. The creature's body stiffened while its head took to jerking about wildly, as though its hunger for the knight's flesh warred with its wariness of his sword. Finally, some limit of restraint broke in the creature's primitive mind, and it exploded into hissing motion, mouth gaped open to reveal row upon row of curved, serrated fangs jutting out at odd angles.

Gabriel waited until the beast was nearly on top of him. Calmly, in a motion practiced thousands of times before, he pivoted aside and slashed his sword in a downward arc, decapitating the reptile. The creature's body ran for a few feet after the head tumbled over the sand, finally collapsing at the ocean's edge with blood spurting from its neck and turning the water red.

As though sharing a single mind, the lizards watching from the beach rushed forward. Dozens of the things shuffled and hissed over the sands. Gabriel planted his feet again and prepared to meet them, but they bypassed him completely and converged instead upon the carcass of their fallen kin.

The first reptiles to reach the scene tore off chunks of flesh and choked them down while the others snapped for the meat. The carcass was devoured in a matter of seconds, but the fighting continued. The beasts rolled and tumbled over each other in a snarling frenzy, their faces, eyes, and fangs glistening with blood. The moment one of the beasts received even a superficial wound, it was set upon from all sides by the others, and taken down hissing in rage to its death.

Gabriel circled around the scene and headed inland. He

stopped when he got to the dunes at the beach's edge and looked back at the chaos. At least a hundred of the beasts now fought. Scores more bellied over the sands from every direction. Sounds of ripping flesh and snapping bone filled the air. From a distance, the writhing mass resembled some primordial, bubbling tar pit from which all the nightmares of the world fought for shape and the right to be born.

Gabriel spat into the sand. After he destroyed Elezear, he swore, he would eradicate every single one of those unclean beasts and burn the whole diseased island to a cinder. The very existence of the place was an affront to Dunrabian and everything that the god stood for. He spit again and turned away.

Beyond the beach, the land turned to hills made of black, jagged stone. Gabriel picked out the highest hill in view and headed toward it, leaving behind a trail of bloody footprints as the sharp edges of the rock cut into his feet.

The wound in his forehead had stopped bleeding, but he could feel his skull beneath the coagulant. A row of indentations lined his ribs where they'd broken. The knight sighed in annoyance at the pain and stopped to deal with the distraction.

Pain mastery was one of the arts of war he'd spent his life perfecting. Pain, the warrior monks taught, was only an illusion. Like desire, like love, like fear, it was just another of humanity's weaknesses and failings. The only real thing was faith. Everything else existed solely to test faith and, through that crucible, to perfect it. A knight's ultimate purpose in life was to dispel all illusions, until faith was the only reality that remained.

He did not resist the pain, nor did he indulge it. He simply closed his eyes and watched it move through his body as though he was far, far above it, disconnected and disinterested. He slowed his breathing, systematically relaxing every muscle, from his face down to his feet. The throbs, aches, and burns faded. They grew more and more distant, like an echo, until finally they were so faint that he did not even notice them, anymore. After that, it was as though they had never been.

Gabriel opened his eyes and continued walking as darkness crept over the hills. The sun had only a narrow circle in the center of the Tempest Gate through which to shine, and it was already dropping beneath the rim of the clouds. The knight quickened his pace.

The rocky terrain softened as he gained elevation. Corrupt, misshapen trees rose up out of the ground and spilled limply onto their sides like the flayed arms of some tortured, subterranean thing that had broken through the surface of the ground just before dying. Thin vines covered in red barbs drooped from the mutant trunks, twisting and curling along red-clay earth like snakes.

Creatures in various stages of decomposition lay entangled within the vines. The stench of rancid meat hung heavy in the humid air. Gabriel eyed the inventory of bizarre corpses with disgust – an eyeless pig with four thick, knuckled fingers at the end of its six appendages; giant rats with suction cups like wet mouths lining their flanks; the yellowed, shrunken carapaces of giant, winged spiders. The vines coiled tighter around the dead things as Gabriel passed, guarding their putrid meals jealously.

The sight disgusted and enraged the knight. It was as though the entire island existed solely to insult life. In all his years of war and missioning in the name of the Church, years that had taken him into terrible battles and wildernesses without name, he had never seen a place so vile, so utterly hopeless.

The knight drew his sword and slashed his way through the vines. He could have simply circumvented them, but he cut zealously instead, happy to see the abominations recoil and shrink from his sword. A black, blood-like substance dripped from their severed parts, pooling in the clay.

He cut a swath through the carnivorous vegetation until

he crested the line of hills and followed the slope downward into a different wood, one of willowy trees with bare canopies sprawling over a floor covered in dead, waxen leaves. The island darkened. Cursing, Gabriel pressed ahead. No moon hung in the sky to provide light. After a few minutes, he could no longer be sure if he headed for the island's interior, or some other direction. He did not want to stop for even a moment now that he stood on the very same island as the demon, but he was becoming lost, and he had only become more lost the longer that he pressed blindly forward.

Gabriel stuck his sword into the ground and knelt before it. He mentally reassured his god that he was not stopping out of sloth, but only to keep from delaying his quest's fulfillment by wandering too far astray. He closed his eyes, pressed his forehead against the flat of the blade, and prayed.

In whispers, he entreated his god. "I have come to rid the world of evil. I promise to give all my heart to this task, and to give my life for the world if necessary, in order to rid it of Elezear. I am nothing. I am only the Arm that wields your Sword, my god. Give me the strength to carry that blade and complete my task." He made a fist and kissed the back of his hand, an ancient gesture of faith passed down for generations through the knight's order. "All light is forged in war with darkness," he said, and kissed his hand once more.

Things moved in the forest all around him. They slithered and crawled through the leaves, stopping just outside the clearing, where they breathed raggedly in the dark. The knight remained still, as though he was sleeping, with the hope that the creatures would come within the arc of his blade so that he could destroy them. Perhaps sensing his intentions, the creatures slinked back into the trees, leaving him in silence. After that, the only sounds that disturbed the night were the distant, scattered shrieks and howls of tortured beasts crying out against the endless rumble of the Tempest Gate.

Part Four

Several times sleep threatened to overtake him, but sleep in that place would be death, so he forced himself to stay awake. As the hours dragged on, he prayed and visualized his coming battle, mentally practicing every parry, every thrust, every feint. Before meeting any adversary on the field of battle, the warrior monks taught, a knight should have already met his enemy a thousand times in his mind.

Still, even with the great self-discipline that he had, Gabriel found his mind drifting to other places. So close now to Elezear, after so many years of waiting, he could not help but think back to the first time he heard the legend of the demon, that one night that had shaped the course of his destiny forever.

He had been just a boy, only ten years old, lying on a thin pile of hay upon the cold, earthen floor of his family's sod hut. He shifted beneath a horse blanket far too small for his long, frail body, so that every time he covered one part of himself, he exposed another. Cold nights seemed to last forever in those days, long hours spent in an endless chase to stay warm.

His drunken father sat cross-legged beside him, swaying back and forth as he stared into the dwindling flames of the hut's stone hearth. Insects crunched in the straw roof overhead. Rats scampered in the shadows, their pink eyes glittering in the firelight.

Gabriel's father was the village storyteller in more ways

than one. In addition to being a bard of some talent, he was also a conman and a liar. The other villagers called him Pinshaw, which was the name of a forest bird that could change the hue of its feathers at will. The bird used its talent for duplicity to sneak amongst other birds and eat their eggs. Like that bird, Gabriel's father knew how to get close enough to people to take the things that mattered most to them.

"Elezear," Pinshaw said, glaring at him with eyes glowing madly in the firelight. "Father of Nightmares they called it. Maggot of Night." He smiled, revealing teeth turned green by the lily wine he favored. Whenever he got drunk, which was the case that night, he delighted in frightening his son. "They called it these names, and all other sorts of nonsense, because they didn't know what it really was. They didn't even know where it came from. They only knew that it did come, and that it left nothing in its wake but ashes and dust."

He took a drink from his wine flask and leaned forward so that his face was within an inch of Gabriel's. For a second it seemed he would fall completely over, but he righted himself at the last moment and continued. When he spoke, the commingled stench of fermented lilies and smoked cronco-weed grew so bad that Gabriel would have recoiled, if not for the whipping such a move would surely have won him.

"It laid the great cities to waste in days. It wiped out whole peoples. The demon took nothing, asked for nothing. It just cut across the countryside, destroying everything it set its sights on. Men, women, little boys such as yourself." He rocked backwards and sneered at his son, measuring the boys' fear. "It didn't matter. It made no difference to Elezear."

Gabriel looked up through a hole in their crumbling roof. The night sky stretched out, vaster and darker than it had ever looked before. For the first time in his life, he saw the sky not as a canopy of beautiful and mysterious lights, but as an endless expanse of nothingness that threatened to swallow the entire world. He shivered. Whether the fear came from Elezear or from his father's drunkenness, he could not be sure. It was probably both.

"The armies of every nation and tribe joined together to fight the demon. They boarded ships and sailed to the island where the thing slept. It was an army the likes of which the world has never seen, neither before, nor since. Yet for all their numbers, they didn't even slow the monster down. Before the sun set on the first day of battle, three of every four warriors that started the campaign lay dead."

Pinshaw snapped his fingers. "Just like that, the great army was defeated, and the world lost. The few poor and dumb bastards that were still alive gathered together for one final charge. It was suicide, but what else is there for men to do in the face of certain death, except to die heroically?" He chuckled at that thought, seeming very pleased with his insight, or perhaps simply amused at the notion of heroism.

"As they began their final charge, Elezear spoke. Its words came into the minds of every person in the world at once." He took a slug of his wine, peering over the skin with narrowed eyes. "Every single person in the world, boy, not only those on the island. Many went mad just at the sound of the demon's voice. A lot more of them wished they'd done so.

"Elezear told them it hadn't come to wage war. It only wanted to give a display of its power so complete, so terrible, that no doubt was left in anyone's mind that it could eradicate the entire human race if it wanted. But it had nothing to gain by that eradication. The demon had no interest in conquest. It only wanted to feed, and Elezear doesn't feed on flesh." He leaned close to the boy again and whispered harshly, "Elezear feeds on souls."

Gabriel gasped, realizing when he did that he'd been

holding his breath. He wanted to hide the fear he knew his father so wanted to see, but his body betrayed him as always, and his hands began to tremble.

Smirking at his son's fright, Pinshaw nodded and continued. "A soul cannot be taken by force. Not even by Elezear. It can only be given willingly by the one who possesses it. If but one person among all of humanity would make that sacrifice, the demon said, it would spare the world. If not, it would wipe out every last trace of the human race, and it would be as if they had never existed at all."

Pinshaw picked up a rusted poker and jabbed it into the embers of the hearth, sending a cloud of sparks bursting out and scattering skyward. Gabriel watched them drift up towards the straw roof, which had been dried by months of drought. He exhaled in relief when their orange lights flickered out before setting the hut on fire.

Jabbing at the embers again, oblivious to the sparks or their threat, Gabriel's father continued. "Milan, the first Holy Knight, stepped forward to make the sacrifice. He climbed the demon's Spire, with everyone that was left from the world's army watching, and disappeared within the cave atop it. Some legends say it happened instantly, others say that it took hours, but what they all agree on is that some point after Milan walked into the cave, a terrible thunder cracked through the sky and the ground shook and broke open in places to swallow any poor fool that had been standing there. After that, neither Milan nor Elezear ever came outside again.

"The few warriors that were still alive sailed back to their homes. Those sorcerers that were still alive stayed behind to work their deviltry together. They cast a spell that surrounded the island with a storm that would never stop blowing. The rain fell so hard that it was like a solid wall keeping the world out. They called it the Tempest Gate, and it stands there to this day."

The Tempest Gate, Gabriel thought with wonder. More than his fear of the demon or the wall guarding it, he felt excitement and intrigue. Warring with a demon might be a terrible thing, but it would be better than shivering in a hut with fleas crawling in his hair while he listened to his drunken father ramble on about the corruption of the world. Just to see such a thing as the Gate, just to make such a journey and fight such a battle, would be better than an entire life spent toiling in the potato fields.

Gabriel was nervous that his excitement would show through in his eyes, but Pinshaw wasn't looking at him. Instead, the man rocked back and forth on the floor, staring into the last of the fire's glowing cinders.

"The great cities were rebuilt," Pinshaw said, slurring his words. "People went back to living their lives, such as they were. Eventually, they learned to live with Elezear in the world. But the Seers made a prophecy that things wouldn't always be so. They said that one day a boy would be born who would become the next Holy Knight. He'd be the greatest hero that ever graced this world, and he'd be blessed with the power to slay Elezear."

His father reeled a moment, squinted into the darkness as though seeing something there for the first time. His eyes went wide as he turned back to stare into his son's face. He reached out and gripped the boy by the shoulder. "Maybe that boy is you."

Pinshaw stared solemnly at Gabriel long enough that he started to believe he had really meant what he said. Just when the boy let his guard down and tentatively smiled, accepting the possibility that he had been singled for a divine purpose, his father burst into laughter. "You're an idiot, boy. The only quest you've got to look forward to is spreading hog shit on the fields. The Seers said all sorts of nonsense and prophesied no end of sheep balls. None of it ever came true. Not a word."

Gabriel's father rocked backwards, caught himself, and then rocked forward to stare into the flames. His eyes fluttered.

He took one more drink of wine, squeezed the skin until no more liquid came out, and slumped over face first onto the floor. Within moments, he began to snore.

Gabriel stayed awake through the night. The fear he had felt at his father's story faded, while the desperate excitement in his heart grew. The details of Elezear's terrible power disappeared from his memory completely. What burned bright in his mind was the prophecy of the boy born to become the Holy Knight. He fantasized that he was that boy, a young warrior clad in gleaming armor as he rode to glory and fame atop a towering steed, wielding the great Sword of Dunrabian, with all the armies of the Church following behind.

Gabriel imagined himself leading the Church to victory over all of its heathen adversaries, imagined himself destroying Elezear and riding home to a whole countryside full of brightly colored banners, celebrators, and adorers, all of them cheering his name. Princesses lined up for a chance to woo him with their beauty and their charms. Kings bent on one knee to promise their very kingdoms to his service. From the first night that he heard the story of Elezear, Gabriel did not see nightmares in the tale. He saw only hope, a glimpse of light in an otherwise dark future.

Born on the lowest social rung of a system without means of upward mobility, divine providence was his only possibility of escape. Peasants worked and died in poverty, and that was all there was to it. There was no reward, no point in aspiration or ambition. For a child raised in such a situation, there was nothing to look forward to but a lifetime of toil. To a peasant boy with no prospects for life outside the dirt expanse of the potato fields, a battle with a demon seemed a meager price to pay for brighter fortunes.

As his father snored beside him, Gabriel watched the cinders die in the hearth. For the first time in his life, he imagined the possibility of a different, brighter future ahead. The moment he grabbed hold of that idea, there was no way he could go back to living without dreams and ambitions again. In the early morning hours, with the first light of dawn breaking over the hills, Gabriel got down on his knees and prayed.

Jeff Suwak

PART FIVE

With the first rays of sunlight shining over the rim of the Tempest Gate, Gabriel pulled his sword from the ground and made his way into the island's interior.

The vegetation thickened as he went. Thorn-covered trees, black as onyx, grew together in a tangled wall. He hacked a path through the snarled mass, but it made for slow going. It would take him a day to move a single mile in that terrain.

After an hour passed and he was lathered in sweat with his head swimming from hunger and heat, the knight hacked through the branches and stumbled forward onto a narrow trail rutted into the ground. The well-worn path extended in both directions as far as he could see. He knelt and examined the copper colored soil for the tracks of whatever creature had made the trail, but it was too heavily eroded for him to identify any markings. He stood, loosened his sword in its sheath, and followed the course.

He followed the meandering trail through the forest for about an hour, until he came to a place where it terminated at the edge of a marsh's brackish water. Continuing over the swamp was a primitive footbridge made of logs and branches, some sodden and looking near to collapse, others composed of more lightly colored wood, indicating recent repairs. Up to that point, the path could have been explained by any number of animals, but the makers of this newer construction clearly possessed human, or at least humanoid, intelligence. Gabriel drew his sword and followed the bridge.

Insects swarmed in the swamp's hot, fetid air. The place stank like the gangrenous flesh of the lepers Gabriel sometimes passed in the city streets. Sunlight broke through the thickly tangled canopy overhead in patches, offering only dim illumination. Malformed trees with bloated trunks grew out of the dark water. Things moved just below the surface—fins, serpentine shapes, clusters of eyes hinting at wicked things beneath.

Mosquitoes the size of Gabriel's fist maneuvered to find parts of his flesh to feast. After swatting one of the insects on his shoulder with his bare hand and winding up with a fistful of goo for his troubles, he took to cutting them out of the air with his sword. Their oversized corpses fell to the rancid water where they were immediately snatched down under the surface by whatever life lurked beneath.

Rounding a thick copse of mangrove trees, Gabriel reached a point where the walkway intersected with another. He stopped. Walking across the intersection, two men carried the carcass of a monstrous snake between them. The scrawny, pale figures had mud-caked beards speckled with pieces of twigs and leaves, and wore sodden rags beneath coats of chain mail with links welded together by rust. They stopped at the sight of the knight and stood watching him with hollow, lifeless eyes.

Gabriel concealed the shock he felt at finding two men in a place where no human beings were supposed to have stepped for five hundred years. Their presence was impossible, he thought. No one was left on the island after the battle with Elezear, and no one but he could have penetrated the Tempest Gate. It was only through the grace of Dunrabian that he had survived.

"Who are you?" Gabriel asked, forcing calm into his voice.

The men looked at each other and then back at Gabriel, as though the question itself perplexed them.

Gabriel sheathed his sword, thinking that perhaps his blade was making them nervous. "Where do you come from?"

The one carrying the snake's head cocked his head in confusion. "We come from home," he said. His tone implied that there was no other answer, no other possible place that anybody could come from.

"What are your names? Surely you have those, at least."

"I am Milfis," the one at the tail answered. "He is Ril."

Gabriel found it strange to hear such names associated with the living. They were ancient monikers written about in the oldest chapters of the Book, and had fallen out of fashion long before the knight was born. They were names of myth and memory. Hearing them used by living men made him feel as though he had traveled into the past.

"Take me to the one that speaks for your people."

The men looked at each other in a long moment of silence, dead eyes swimming in their pale faces. Nothing was said and no expressions passed, yet Gabriel had the feeling that they were communicating with each other. Simultaneously they broke their gazes, and Milfis looked back to the knight. "Who are you?"

"I am Gabriel." When the men did not seem to recognize the name, he added, "Holy Knight, Arm of the Sword of Dunrabian."

The men looked at each other again. If they exchanged any kind of signal, it was too subtle for Gabriel to see, but they both seemed to arrive at a conclusion at the same time. They turned at once to face him. "You have to speak to Gogol."

"Take me to him," Gabriel commanded, but the men had already turned and started down the walkway with the snake in their arms. Their impertinent attitudes were frustrating. People did not simply give the Holy Knight orders and then walk away, as though taking for granted the fact that he would obey them. The inexplicability of their existence helped him hold back a rebuke, and he followed them over the walkway that cut through the marsh.

He watched the corpse of the dead serpent drag along the trail as they went. It was white as sun-bleached bone and covered along the entirety of its flank with pink, oozing sores. The men carrying the snake were separated from each other by three or four feet, yet the monster's tail end still dragged a long ways behind them.

"What do you plan to do with that snake?" Gabriel asked, suspecting the answer already, but hoping he was wrong.

"Eat it," Ril said, as though the answer was obvious and the question foolish.

Gabriel shook his head in revulsion, eyeing the puss-rimmed sores. What manner of men would consume such a thing? *Maybe they're Elezear's servants*, he thought, glancing over his shoulder to make sure he wasn't being followed.

Something moving in the back of Milfis's head caught Gabriel's attention. After a moment, he realized he was looking at tiny worms swarming in the man's hair. Maybe they weren't men at all, he reasoned. Maybe they were some form of undead, the walking corpses of those thousands that Elezear had killed. There were stories in the Book of such things.

The walkway led out of the swamp and into a narrow valley cutting through sheer, sandstone cliffs. It climbed several feet between the valley's orange walls before entering into a wide bowl eroded into the rocky terrain. Several houses stood within the space. They were built of rough, unworked stone, with roofs and doors made from thatched branches that had been bleached white by the elements. At the center of the houses stood a rectangular lodge, much larger than the others, built from red stones that had been smoothed and fitted with greater care than the lesser habitations.

A woman dressed in a soiled, tattered slip came to the doorway of the house closest to the trail and watched them enter the village. She scratched absentmindedly at the one breast hanging out of a torn patch in her clothes. Two children, naked and covered with dirt, appeared at her sides. All three had the same wasted eyes as Milfis and Ril, but there was something more terrible about that look in the eyes of children. Gabriel bowed to them as he passed. They did not return his greeting, but just stared after him in an eerie mixture of wonder and suspicion.

Women and children, too, the knight thought, shaking his head. The conditions of the island were not good enough for dogs, much less people, yet there were women and children living there. If they were not agents of Elezear, then he would rescue them all from that place as soon as he destroyed the demon. If he had to sail back through the Tempest Gate himself and load every one of those pitiful people upon his craft alone, he would save them. Life in that place was a punishment that no one deserved.

Two men emerged from one of the houses and helped carry off the snake. Milfis left the group and led Gabriel through the rows of primitive huts to the central lodge. "Wait here," the man said, his words barely audible, as though he was too exhausted to attain full volume. "I'll tell Gogol you're here."

As Gabriel waited for Milfis' return, villagers emerged from their houses to follow the serpent-bearers. They formed a kind of sickly parade, dragging their bare and filthy feet through the dust after their putrid meal. But they did not all follow. Several men remained behind, standing in the shadows with knives and clubs in their hands, watching.

Gabriel's guide emerged from the lodge. "Gogol will see you now," he said, and walked off down the path.

Before stepping inside the door, Gabriel looked once more at the armed observers lurking in the darkness. He held his eyes for a moment on each of them, letting them know he saw them and was not afraid. Resting his hand on the handle of his sword, he turned and entered the lodge.

The interior of the lodge was a single, windowless, and dirt-floored room, filled with wooden bookshelves bursting with books and parchments. Sunlight beamed through gaps in the wall-stones, creating pale arcs of light swarming with dust motes. The bright shafts crisscrossed through the dark space like a luminous web. At the center of the web was a throne made of human skulls. A torch flickered beside the grim seat and lighted a man standing before it on a path that had been lightly rutted into the earthen floor, as though by decades of restless pacing in circles.

A willowy beard flowed over the man's full suit of plate mail armor like an ancient, moth eaten tapestry. A corroded metal band, the last remains of a decomposed crown, sat upon his bald head. The torch and the crisscrossing arcs of light sent strange shadows curling over the old man's features, so that it was as if his face had no definite shape.

Dozens of enormous, spiny tarantulas swarmed over his breastplate, yet they were not the thing that brought Gabriel to an abrupt halt. Instead, it was the image hammered into the breast of his armor. Still visible beneath the dents and blotches of rust was an image of a unicorn rearing into the air with a three-headed snake impaled upon its horn. Such was the symbol of the Church of Dunrabian.

Gabriel gasped. "Who are you to wear that mark?"

"I am Gogol," the man replied. "I was born to wear this mark, from the start of my days, to the very end." A tarantula scurried over his shoulder and disappeared beneath his beard.

"You speak for the people outside?"

"No one speaks for our people, for there is no one to speak to. But I am the king, such as a king can be in this place, and more comfortable with words than the others. You come from the world?" He said 'world' as though it were the name of some city or country.

Gabriel nodded. "I come from the world."

"Yet you do not know this symbol on my breast?"

"I know the symbol well, only not how you've come to wear it."

Gogol looked confused. "Has the world truly forgotten so much of this island's story?"

Gabriel threw his head back proudly and scoffed. "On the contrary, I have known the story of this island since I was a boy."

Gogol's thin lips curled back in a bitter smile. "I have *lived* the story of this island since I was a boy, my friend. Forgive me if I am unimpressed by your scholasticism." He leaned forward and waved the knight forward. "Step closer. I wish to see what men from the world look like."

Gabriel stepped within the illumination of the torch. Gogol looked him up and down. "Do all the people of the world now forego the wearing of clothes?"

The knight looked down at his bare chest and feet. "I had to give them up, or else drown." He was unaccustomed to being treated so lightly, and struggled to contain his anger. Princes bowed in his presence. Knights took off their helmets and stared at their feet in deference when he walked by. They certainly would not inquire so casually about his nakedness.

"Are there any others with you?"

"No."

"Was your ship blown off course?"

"I came here by intention," Gabriel said. He tapped the hilt of his sword. "I have come to slay the demon Elezear."

Gogol laughed the strange, wheezing cackle of a man not at all practiced in doing so. Soon he fell into a fit of violent coughing. Catching his breath, he asked, "Have you come also to spear the sun? Will you drink up the ocean while you are at it? All the armies of the world could not defeat the demon. Is your sword arm mightier than all of them?"

Gabriel bristled under the man's mockery. "It's clear you have been absent from the world for some time, so I will forgive your ignorance, but you would do well to know that I am not some squire or messenger boy to be mocked. I am Gabriel, the Holy Knight, Arm of the Sword of Dunrabian."

Gogol's eyes flashed with a strange illumination, as though a lantern had passed behind them. When he spoke, his voice was so strained it sounded like a hiss. "There was but one Holy Knight, and he gave his life long ago, so that the world may live."

Gabriel shook his head. "You are wrong. I am the Holy Knight, and it is my duty to destroy Elezear."

Gogol pointed at the unicorn on his breastplate. "And it is my duty, and the duty of all those here, to ensure that no one ever disturbs it."

"You protect the beast?" Gabriel grabbed hold of his sword and wheeled about, ready to draw as he scanned the shadows of the lodge for attackers.

Gogol glanced down at the partially drawn weapon disinterestedly. "We are the protectors of all humanity. Of all the world. Have you truly never heard of the Milanites?"

Gabriel relaxed his grip, but still kept his hand on his sword's hilt. "I don't know what game you are playing at, nor where you have come from, but there is no mention of such people in the Book." He scoffed. "In fact, I've heard no mention of such people anywhere."

Gogol gestured at the room around him. "And yet, here we are, as we have been for five hundred years, ensuring that Elezear is not disturbed." He made a fist and kissed the back of his hand. "So that the world may live."

Gabriel shifted in uncertainty. Gogol and his people were

clearly mad, if not outright agents of darkness, yet something in the old man's voice bothered him. The tone wasn't one of lies or delusions. Gabriel recognized faith and conviction when he heard them, for they were things more familiar to him than anything else in the world.

"Even if your story is true, which I do not believe, your people should be celebrating my arrival. After I destroy the beast, you will be free to return to the world."

"If we are ever free," Gogol said, "there will be no world left to return to. Elezear is not some dragon to be slain. It is something much, much more terrible than that."

Gabriel bristled under the old man's lecture. His rightful position as the Holy Knight was something that no one, not even the High Ecclesiastic Nimphus, ever openly challenged. He straightened up and thrust his shoulders back proudly. "You don't know who I am, and because of that, I will forgive your ignorance. But I assure you that I don't take my mission lightly. I have spent my life preparing for this quest."

Gogol waved off the words as if they were a child's nonsensical babblings. "And we have spent our lives carrying out ours. Through the entirety of our days, we live and die by our duty, and nothing else. Please understand if I do not fall to your feet in reverence."

Gabriel felt his face tick under the insult, but retained his composure. "What is this duty you speak of?"

Gogol let out a long, sad exhale. "It pains me to learn that you do not know of our sacrifice." He stared at the floor, suddenly looking even older than before. "You know of Milan, yes?"

"Of course. He sacrificed his soul so that the demon would spare the world."

"That is true. But that is not the end of the story." Gogol walked to the bookshelves standing in the shadows along the wall. He picked through the tattered parchments and tomes that filled them until he located a cracked, leather bound book. He took it down. "For us, it was only the beginning. The pact was not finished with Milan. It was only started with him, and it must continually be honored if the world's pardon is to be extended."

Gabriel struggled to comprehend what the man was saying. He understood the words, but could not grasp their implications. Or, he thought, perhaps the problem was that he did comprehend them perfectly clearly, but did not want to. "Are you saying that you continue to feed the thing?"

Gogol shuffled back with the book in his hands and laid it out over the throne. "Yes. So that the world may live."

An indignant rage surged through Gabriel. He reached the throne in two long strides to jab a finger into Gogol's breastplate. "That is blasphemy of the worst order. What kind of men would do such a thing?"

"Wise ones," Gogol answered, looking down at Gabriel's finger in disdain. His eyes flared with sudden intensity. "You dare cast judgment on those without whom you would not even be alive to judge? We suffer this fate, and we watch our children suffer this fate, day after day after day, all of our lives, so that a world that has forgotten us can continue to exist."

The man's frail body shook with rage. "We have nothing to sustain our spirits other than the stories of the world beyond the Tempest Gate, the paradise that we are preserving. The horror of this place does not lessen through the generations. We are born exhausted by its desolation, and die exhausted by its desolation."

"Then let me free you from this nightmare!" Gabriel shouted, surprised at the desperation he heard in his own voice. He did not understand how the ragged, decrepit king could be so blind to his divine favor or to his power. It had always been obvious to others.

"You do not understand," Gogol said, trembling with anger. "You would not be here in the first place if you did. There are things, knight, which are older than men, older even than the world itself. They are woven into the very fabric of life from threads of some greater design that we were never meant to understand. Such things cannot be destroyed. They were not meant to be destroyed. It is nothing more than a sickness of vanity and hubris to believe that any man's life has been made exempt from their immutable law. Elezear is one of those things. It was here before the world took its form, and it will be here long after."

Gabriel started to argue, but could not find the words. He had no fear of Gogol, or of Gogol's people, but the king's refusal to acknowledge his station bothered him. He could not explain why it vexed him so badly, but that did nothing to change the fact that it did. Unsettled by his unfamiliar vulnerability, he tried to mask it with bravado. "I have seen the men of this place. They are barely men. They cannot stop me."

Gogol studied him from beneath a heavy brow. "Perhaps not," he said. "But we will all die trying." He opened the book on the seat of the throne and pointed to its pages. "I'm trying to talk reason into you. My concern is not for the Milanites. Death is the one luxury that we have to look forward to. No one here would fight one second for their own life. I'm only trying to stop you from destroying your own world, and your own people. There is nothing for me to gain by doing so. My only concern is honoring the duty my ancestors swore to uphold."

Gabriel examined the tome. Its yellow pages were brittle and cracked. The words were of the same ancient language as the one that the Book was written in. It was a formal alphabet that was used only for writing, not speaking, and had not been employed for centuries. Only those in the Church's order learned how to read it. Whatever other tricks might be at work, the book spread out on the throne truly was an ancient one. Gabriel stood before the tome and read by flickering torchlight the passage that Gogol had selected. It read:

Milan, the Holy Knight, entered the cave atop the Spire and offered his soul to the foul, blighted thing called Elezear. Lightning rent the sky and the ground shook and ripped open and swallowed people up into the darkness at the heart of the world. After the screaming stopped, a long silence settled over the island.

In that deep silence, won as it was by Milan's courage and virtue, the demon spoke again. This time, it agreed to rest and to leave the affairs of humanity alone forever, so long as humanity would continue feeding it. One soul per year, the demon demanded. One soul to preserve the pattern of human existence.

Inspired by the heroism of the great Milan, fifty men and fifty women stepped forth from the armies of the world to fulfill the bargain humanity made with the demon. These one hundred people agreed to live on the island for the rest of their lives, bearing children, and offering one soul per year in sacrifice to Elezear. In return, the demon would keep to its dark nest and spare the world its wrath. The champions that agreed to this sacrifice were called Milanites. They were the true followers of the Holy Knight's example.

Each of the volunteers understood when they stepped forward that they were dooming themselves to lives of woe and agony, hunger and darkness. There was no reward for them, no treasure or glory. The world beyond might know of their deed, but it would be too far away to ever show any gratitude.

I, scribe of the Milanites, and one blessed to

stand amongst this Noble Hundred, have been given the task of recording this day. This tale is to be handed down, generation by generation, to be memorized by every member of our order. Let this story be passed from ear to ear until the end of all time, so that no Milanite ever doubts the importance of their sacrifice.

Our place is not one of pleasures of the flesh, nor is it one of glory. Our place is to give up our lives so that the world may live. This tale is to be read, spoken, and sung, until the end of time, so that none of our people ever doubts the importance of their fate. It is we who keep the demon at bay. It is we who spare the world of its wrath.

In honor of the Holy Knight Milan, who gave his soul so that the world may live, let no one who is given this grave and noble task forget why they are here. The wizards will complete their spell soon and surround the island with the Tempest Gate. From that point on, no one may enter, and no one may leave. The world of humanity will be cleaved in half, divided by the Gate into two separate fates. To one goes the happiness of life. To the other goes the honor of defending it.

Gabriel's head reeled. He nearly reached out to brace himself against Gogol, but managed to restrain the impulse. The passage he had read could not be true. There were no mistakes in the Book. There could not be, especially not in the story of Elezear. If one part of the Book was mistaken, then every other part was put into doubt. It implied the possibility that the prophecy of the Vision itself was false, and if that Vision was false, then everything about Gabriel was a lie.

His mouth turned dry. He tried to swallow, but couldn't. The possibility stood before him that the Book's stories were mistaken and he was never anything at all besides a poor peasant boy, which would make him on that day nothing more than a fool with a sword. He bit down so hard his teeth ached. It could not be true. It was impossible. Why, then, did it make him tremble?

Gabriel turned and sneered at Gogol, repeating a familiar line of Church wisdom. "The lies of the unfaithful come in many bindings, but truth comes in only one. That one true text is known as the Book. I've read that Book so many times that its words and its lessons are inscribed on the walls of my heart. I can tell you, without the slightest of doubts, that this tome you have set before me is not that Book, and so is a tome of lies."

Gogol hung his head sadly and let out a long sigh. His expression did not change in the slightest as he drew forth a thin, rusty dirk from behind his back and lunged forward. Gabriel flung himself aside, narrowly avoiding the blade. Gogol, his frail body animated by some inner fire, stalked forward, eyes gleaming with fanatic purpose.

Gabriel drew his sword as he backpedaled. He wanted to talk sense into Gogol, to calm the situation and avoid any bloodshed, but the king moved relentlessly forward, stabbing his dirk out before him as he probed for the knight's throat. The attack left no time for negotiations.

Gabriel backed into a bookshelf and the aged king's blade nearly caught him in the eye. Ducking and pivoting aside, knowing that the strike had come too close for him to allow the scenario to continue, he slashed Gogol's neck open.

The decrepit king fell to his knees. Despite clutching his throat with one hand and gasping soundlessly for air, he continued to hold the dirk out before him, stabbing pointlessly at the air in Gabriel's direction. Bright red blood pumped out through the cracks between his fingers.

"So that the world may live," the king wheezed, and pitched forward onto the floor, his plate mail armor landing with a hollow thud.

Gabriel sheathed his sword. He kicked the dirk out of Gogol's hand and rolled the man onto his back. The king's eyes stared vacantly into the rafters of the lodge. Tarantulas scattered from beneath his beard and scurried in all directions over the floor. Gabriel pressed the man's eyes gently shut and crossed his arms over his chest in a knight's burial position.

"Forgive him, Dunrabian," he prayed. "Though he was led astray, he believed that he was doing your service. Please find a place for him in your hall. He was lost and confused, but he was brave, too, and loyal in his own way."

Gabriel stood and looked down at the dead king. A nagging thread of uncertainty tugged at his mind. The Book was supposed to be complete, yet there was no mention in it of the Milanites, nor of any people living on the island. The inconsistency lent Gogol's words a measure of truth, no matter how hard the knight tried to deny it. He looked to the tome lying on the throne, everything about the object screaming that it was authentic.

He looked back to the corpse, feeling for a moment like some lowly assassin that came over the sea to cut the pitiful old man down in his own home. He shook his head against that shameful notion. He was the Holy Knight, and he existed only to carry out Dunrabian's will. Consequently, everything he did was justified by the very fact that he had done it. Gogol, and Gogol's people, had been placed there to test his resolve and his faith, just like everything else in the world. And, just like every test before, he had passed.

Gabriel turned from the dead king and took the torch from its sconce. By its light, he located a flint in a box beside the throne. He stamped out the torch's flame and took down the faded, linen banner that hung from one of the walls. In faded red stitches was sewn the unicorn of the Church impaling a three headed snake on its horn.

Gabriel wrapped the torch and the flint into the banner and knotted the makeshift sack onto his belt. The knight looked down on Gogol one more time. The gash stretched across the king's neck looked like some sort of deranged smile, an evil mouth laughing darkness, blood, and the promise of eternal terror. Gabriel could not shake the unnerving feeling that the dead man had gotten the last laugh. What the joke might have been, Gabriel could not guess.

PART SIX

The image of the dead king's features summoned the memory of another. Gabriel tried to force the picture out of his thoughts, but he could not. In his mind, superimposed over Gogol's face, was the glassy-eyed visage of the monk Alger, his mouth twisted open in a gaping sneer as he stared breathlessly into the air. Weeks after the monk's passing, that image remained seared into Gabriel's brain.

Alger, the oldest monk in the order, was already ancient when Gabriel first arrived at the Church as a boy. He was known as a kind man of unbending integrity, and a person whose nature was diametrically opposed to politics. In that way, Alger and Gabriel had something in common, but that was the definitive end of the similarities they might share.

Alger's peers often gossiped amongst themselves about how the only thing preventing the monk from rising higher in the ranks was his obstinate refusal to compromise or negotiate. He spent endless hours in the library honing his seemingly ageless mind, and perhaps because of that investment, he was never shy about expressing his opinions or offering his knowledge. Many people suffered the wrath of Alger's unflinching straightforwardness, and Gabriel was no exception. The old man's lectures usually ended up being useful words of guidance, and for all their bluster they came from a caring heart. But he reserved a special rancor for the future Holy Knight, and for all his remonstrations, he never once showed the boy any paternal sympathy.

From the start, Alger did everything he could to slow Gabriel's rise. On three separate occasions he called for official Church courts and presented his case against the Holy Knight, using arguments bolstered by precedents he had culled from obscure legal texts. All three cases were ruled out immediately, but each one sent ripples throughout the social landscape for weeks to follow.

Alger's displeasure of the Holy Knight never let up for a moment. His campaign to tarnish Gabriel's' reputation was ceaseless, and his rancor never dulled. When Gabriel passed the other Church figures, they would bow their heads and divert their eyes in reverence to him. In those moments, Alger's face alone could be seen above the crowd, scowling in defiant contempt.

The monk's furious opposition of Gabriel's authority took on new heights after Nimphus approved the knight's request to hunt Elezear. It was a wonder that Alger was even still alive, much less mounting an attack against the Holy Knight and all his supporters, being then well past a hundred years old. Yet, the energy that the monk brought to bear was enough to fill younger men with envy and embarrassment.

As Gabriel's petition for his quest to kill Elezear gained momentum and seemed to become all but inevitable, Alger even went as far as challenging the legitimacy of Gabriel's claim to the title of Holy Knight. It was an act of outrageous disrespect that few people, even those in the Church's highest orders, would have publicly undertaken. If it were not for the fact that Alger was the eldest of the monks, and one so highly respected, it could very well have gotten him banished forever.

Gabriel never understood why the monk despised him. Several times he tried to talk with the man, but Alger wouldn't even answer. Veilhelm, another of the elder monks and a confidant of Alger's, explained once after drinking too much wine that his colleague was enraged at what he called Gabriel's 'arrogant humility and megalomaniacal selflessness.'

Gabriel laughed with Veilhelm at Alger's assessment. It was illogical for a man to be simultaneously arrogant and humble, or megalomaniacal and selfless, and the old monk's mind was clearly deteriorated. Yet, while the knight shrugged off the comments publicly, he continued to be irked by them. His devotion was beyond reproach, his faith unmatched by anyone in the Church. No one, he decided, had the right to question his motivations. The proof of his commitment to Dunrabian was clear for anyone to see.

Whenever there was a religious fast, Gabriel went twice as long without food as anyone else. Whenever the Rite of Penance was observed, Gabriel carried a stone twice as heavy as any other, and carried it twice as far. He spent every Rest Day alone in his chamber praying to Dunrabian. He did all these things despite the fact that he had less than anyone else to pay penance for, and they all knew it. He did not chase women, he did not drink, and he did not lie or steal. He spent every moment of his life acting as a beacon of light for others to follow, training his body for service to his god, acting as an example of what true devotion can achieve. He did it all in the hopes of inspiring others to greater heights of service.

Despite all of that, Alger refused to acknowledge Gabriel's sacrifice or his heroism. He defamed the knight's exploits as acts of narcissism, not religious devotion. The old man even proclaimed that, contrary to being proof of Gabriel's status as Dunrabian's chosen, his feats were proof that Gabriel could not possibly be the Holy Knight. Arrogance, Alger explained, was a sin that the true Holy Knight would be incapable of.

Most of the others in the Church ignored Alger's

complaints and derisions. Over time, he came to be seen as a half-senile, fanatical relic from a phase of the Church's history that had long past. The power of Dunrabian's armies was growing every day, and would soon solidify its hold on the Five Kingdoms. Everyone knew that most of the success was due to Gabriel's presence.

Each of the Holy Knights' battlefield victories validated the Book's decree that the entire world rightfully belonged to Dunrabian's faithful. Attendance at religious services increased in both number and fervor. Young men no longer went into the hills to hide from conscription, but instead willingly joined the war efforts, sometimes walking hundreds of miles just to win the opportunity to serve. Gabriel gave the common people a hero to admire, and someone to believe in. For those gifts, they were willing to die under his banner.

In time, Gabriel told himself that Alger's attacks were motivated by simple jealousy, the last attempts of an unhappy old man to lash out at a younger, stronger prodigy. He knew the old man's fierce integrity well enough to never fully believe in that story, but jealousy made more sense than anything else he could think of, and he often salved his wounded ego with that explanation.

Whatever the motivation for the slander, Gabriel watched Alger closely, especially after the monk's attempts to publicly discredit the quest to kill Elezear. Whether the danger posed by the old man was severe or not, the Book taught that it was a sin to be careless while in service to Dunrabian.

The forces of darkness often employ subversive agents, the Book explained. *These agents prefer slyness over strength, for strength comes from conviction and faith, qualities which the unfaithful do not possess.*

Gabriel's quest was too important to accept even the minor risk of a doddering old man full of delusional ideals, so he took seriously the news that Alger had ridden off in the middle of the night, only hours after Nimphus approved the quest to destroy Elezear. The Holy Knight gathered a handful of his most loyal soldiers and instructed them to keep their ears open for any stories of where the monk went.

Witnesses said Alger rode south. South could have meant any number of places, of course, but Gabriel had a disconcerting feeling from the very start that he knew exactly where Alger had gone. He would have taken off in pursuit himself, but the preparations for his journey had already begun. The battle was too close to slow things down, so he continued working, and waited.

On the eve of his departure, while he knelt on his stone floor praying, Gabriel heard a knock at his door. He opened it to find the young guard Sergis standing with his hazel eyes very wide. Sweat beaded along his upper lip as he fought to steady his breath.

"Master Alger rode into the gate in a frantic hurry, Sir Gabriel," Sergis said. "He went to the High Ecclesiastic's chambers, demanding to speak to him. The soldiers there told him that the High Ecclesiastic left for Church business in the morning. Master Alger didn't believe them until he fought his way into the chambers and saw it for himself. He seemed terribly bothered by something. If I had to describe it, I'd even say he was terrified, almost to the point of hysteria."

Gabriel steadied his breathing to keep the nervousness out of his voice. "When will Nimphus be back?"

"The High Ecclesiastic has ridden out to the eastern plains and won't back until tomorrow at the earliest."

Gabriel let out a sigh of relief. He might have done so too loudly, for the guard seemed to notice and squinted at him quizzically. He collected himself and patted the young man on the shoulder. "Thank you. You've done your duty well. I was concerned for Alger's safety. His old mind isn't the same as it once was, I'm afraid, and I'm relieved to hear that he's home. Now, go back to your post. For all his erratic behavior, it sounds like the Church is safe from Alger's antics for now."

The guard grinned, nodded, and walked off down the hall. Gabriel closed the door. He stood listening to the soldier's footsteps echoing down the passageway. After they faded out of range, he bolted into the hall and ran to Alger's chamber.

"What do you want?" The monk stood in the doorway, face scrunched up in loathing as though he smelled something foul. His lower lip quivered and trembled in the peculiar way it had taken to over the last couple of years.

"I've come to check on your health, Esteemed Father," Gabriel said.

Alger sneered. "More likely to see where I've been, you venomous little snake. Don't 'Esteemed Father' me. I know your secret now."

Gabriel glanced up and down the hallway to see if anyone else had heard the old man's words. Seeing no one, he spoke in a voice barely above a whisper. "What secret are you talking about, Esteemed Father?"

"I went to the village where you were born." The monk smiled, pausing a moment to let his words sink in. "I've never been in that part of the country before, so you can imagine my surprise when I ran into an old friend of mine. A man named Thusis. Do you remember him?" Alger's smile widened for a moment and then abruptly disappeared, like a crocodile snapping its mouth shut. "He remembers you quite well."

Gabriel opened his mouth to answer, but no words came.

"Old Thusis was once a promising servant of the Church." Alger nodded. "Yes, he climbed as high as the Upper Council, in fact. Some even said that one day he would become the High Ecclesiastic. That was before his wits began to leave him, however. Poor man. Eventually, his mind got so bad that he couldn't perform his duties anymore. Of course, that was only after he'd been made privy to the Church's deepest secrets. He knew everything there was to know about our religion, our history, and our Book." Alger's eyes bored into Gabriel's.

"Obviously, a man of such loose thinking as Thusis couldn't be allowed to walk around with such vital, potentially dangerous knowledge. So, though it pained them greatly, the other Ecclesiastics and monks were planning to lock poor Thusis away in some remote tower in the wilderness. But it turns out that Thusis had more of his wits left than people realized. He suspected something was afoot, and knew he had to flee. Before anyone could get their hands on him, he disappeared into the night. I always wondered where old Thusis went. Now I know."

Gabriel cleared his throat. "An amazing story, Esteemed Father. I knew Thusis, though not as well as he seems to have told you. My father told me he was mad and ordered me to stay far away from him. He always seemed like a kind man to me, though. How is he today?"

"His mind is terribly scattered, of course, but he still has his marvelous talent for telling stories. He told me a very interesting one while I visited with him, in fact. It was about a young boy named Gabriel that once lived in the village." Alger cocked his head to one side, grinning as though amused at Gabriel's discomfort.

"This young Gabriel liked to stop by Thusis' home to listen to his stories. The boy loved all the stories of knights and adventures, Thusis said, but there was one story in particular that he wanted to hear, over and over again. My old friend told me that no matter how many times he retold the story, the boy always wanted to hear it once more.

"This favorite story was the one about the Vision that Dunrabian would visit upon the child that would one day become the Holy Knight. You see, Thusis had been informed of this Vision while he was still in the Upper Council. It's funny, the way that certain things are lost to madness, and others are not." Alger feigned deep contemplation on the matter.

"But, this boy named Gabriel, Thusis tells me, simply loved to hear the story. The boy listened so many times that he even took to reciting it himself. He'd sit at Thusis' side and repeat the Vision word for word, asking Thusis to make sure that he had gotten every single detail right. It was almost as if he was studying lessons for a test."

Gabriel checked up and down the hall one more time to make sure that no guards were around. He grabbed Alger by the collar and pushed him back into the room, slamming the door shut behind him.

"Let me explain, Esteemed Father."

Alger's face flushed red. For a moment, it seemed as though it might pop. The quivering of his lower lip worsened, making an audible flapping sound against the upper. "You dare to accost an elder?"

"I don't do it for myself," Gabriel stammered. "Nothing I do is for me. It's all for the Church, for Dunrabian. Can't you see that?"

"You can explain all of this to the Council, after I tell them what I've found." Alger tried to push his way past Gabriel, but the knight did not budge.

"I can't let you do this, Esteemed Father. I must do my duty for the Church. Can't you see that this is all part of Dunrabian's plan? Thusis was the vehicle through which Dunrabian delivered the Vision to me. His role is not proof against my claim to the title of Holy Knight, but proof of its legitimacy. It was all part of the godly design. Haven't my accomplishments thus far proven that I must be the rightful, prophesied Holy Knight? No ordinary man could achieve the things I've achieved. It's only through the will of Dunrabian that I've done so."

Alger scoffed. He spit on the knight's boots. "There never

was a prophesied child. It was all a lie from the very beginning."

Gabriel took step back, stunned at hearing such a blasphemous statement from a venerable member of the Church. His hand lifted on its own accord to strike the elder, but he restrained it before actually doing so. The old man's mind must be farther gone than anyone suspected, he decided. Only a heretic or an imbecile would so besmirch the Vision.

"Listen to yourself," Gabriel said, lowering his hand from its striking position to grip the monk warmly by the shoulder. "Think about what you're saying, Alger. The prophecy is written in the Book, for all the eyes of the world to see. How can you say that it never happened? Does such a thing strike you as the words of a man with an ordered mind?"

Alger shucked the hand off his shoulder. "Don't speak to me like I'm some half-wit. I've spent three of your lifetimes in this Church. I know more of its history than anyone under its roof, including Nimphus. While he and the others spent their lives playing at their little political games and cavorting about in their pompous ceremonies, I was in the library studying the ancient texts. There are books there that no living man has read but me. That is how I have always known you were a charlatan. A liar. There never was a Vision."

"Then what do you call the prophecy that is written so clearly in the Book, for all in the world to see?"

Alger chuckled. "The so called 'prophecy' was nothing more than an invention drummed up to save the Church. People stopped believing in Dunrabian after Elezear nearly destroyed the world. How could they have faith in the salvation promised by a god that couldn't even defeat the evils of this mortal world? Something needed to be done to win the people back, so the Seers invented a story promising that Dunrabian would one day grant a new Holy Knight the power to destroy Elezear and lead the Church to new glory.

It was all nonsense and children's tales, and so it worked. The people returned to the Church in numbers greater than ever before. The armies grew, the power grew, and the priests involved in the conspiracy took the secret to their graves, not even passing it on to those that inherited their positions. It would have been forgotten forever if one of those men hadn't written about it in his journal and hidden that journal away in the bowels of the library for me to find. Some part of him must have been unable to let the truth die from the world completely."

Gabriel could think of nothing to say at first. He stood staring at the old monk, knowing that the words rang true, yet unable to accept them. "If this story is true, why didn't you ever speak of it before?"

Alger straightened out his robe and ran a hand through the wisps of gray hair still clinging to his head like shreds of cotton. "Because the Church, for all its lies, is necessary, just as the Book is necessary. Without them, there would be no order in men or in cities. The Church's lies lift the beasts out of the mud and give them the chance to be something else. Even with all its faults, the world is better off with the lies than without them. Until today, that is, when a single fool threatens the whole world with his delusions of heroism. Now, let me pass, and face what is coming to you."

Alger pushed again at the knight, but Gabriel blocked him. The monk tried to move around the other side, but Gabriel blocked that, too.

"How dare you imprison one of your elders?" Alger shouted and swung at Gabriel's head. The knight dodged the feeble blows and held the monk back at arm's length.

"Calm down, Esteemed Father. I don't want to imprison you, nor do I want to hurt you, but you've gone too far. My quest is at hand. I can't let anyone stop me from fulfilling Dunrabian's will. Your story is plainly madness. I slayed the giant Emir. I defeated the barbarian tribes, and rid the world of dragons. The proof of my rightful position is in the deeds I have done."

Alger tried more desperately to push his way past the knight. He lost his balance in the struggle and tripped over the hem of his robes, falling back onto the floor. Sputtering in rage, he used the wall to pull himself to his feet, spitting out a line or profanities that Gabriel did not think the Church's monks ever heard, much less put into practice.

In the middle of his verbal tirade, Alger choked. The color drained from his face and he winced in pain. He clutched his robe at the area above his left shoulder. Strangely, his usually quavering lip became perfectly still, but the rest of his body started trembling violently. Alger looked at the knight with an expression that could have been disgust or confusion, or both, and collapsed to the floor.

Gabriel reached down to help the monk, but then stopped himself. Looking over his shoulder to make sure the door was still closed, he stood up, and watched the man flounder. If Dunrabian willed that Alger died that night, he decided, then he would not intervene.

He stood over the old man as the monk's breathing slowed and grew ever shallower. The hand clutching at the robes above his heart loosened its grip. His cloudy eyes turned to the sky as he let out a long, ragged sigh. His lips curling back into a silent scream, and he went limp. Gabriel waited several minutes to make sure the man was dead. When he was certain, he left and walked back to his own chamber.

After the shock of the event passed, anger rushed through him. It was wrong that an old man that had served faithfully as a servant to the Church should die so unceremoniously. He deserved better than to be disposed of that way. Gabriel caught himself condemning the actions his god and fell to his knees in shame. He closed his eyes and prayed for forgiveness.

"Forgive me for my weakness and impertinence, Dunrabian," he said. "I never should have doubted your will. I thank you for striking Alger down before he could endanger my quest. I understand that this final act was your way of proving, once and for all, that I am indeed your Holy Knight, and that destroying the Elezear is what you want from me. Though I never doubted the truth of my mission, I now feel renewed conviction. You've shown me such great favor by sacrificing a servant as venerable as Alger. Please hold a place for him in your kingdom, and forgive him for his hubris."

He had planned to sleep for a couple hours that night, but decided that he would stay awake and pray instead, paying penance for his condemnation of Dunrabian. Still, as the light of dawn stretched over the horizon and filtered through his window, Gabriel found himself wondering why his god did not handle the problem differently.

Dunrabian could have simply destroyed the journal before Alger ever found it. He could have struck the monk blind so that he couldn't read, or taken Thusis' voice so he couldn't tell his tale to the monk. There were thousands of possible courses of action other than killing the man.

In the end, Gabriel decided there was no point in trying to understand. Men cannot grasp the complex workings of Dunrabian's mind, he reminded himself. Their place was only to listen, and to obey.

PART SEVEN

Gabriel made his way around the back of Gogol's lodge, trying to appear casual. One of the Milanites emerged from between two houses to walk towards the dead king's chamber while others milled about in the shadows. Grasping crude weapons, they eyed the knight warily.

Gabriel quickened his pace. He moved in the direction opposite from the one he'd arrived in, heading deeper into the island and, hopefully, closer to Elezear. He did not like the idea of fleeing from the rabble of that place, but he also did not wish to have more of their blood on his hands. They were the victims of that cursed island, and the knight only wanted to liberate them.

Halfway to the edge of town, Gabriel looked back to see Milanites gathering in the street. Men, women, and children alike paraded down the row in a staggered trot wielding rusted blades, rocks, and sharpened bones. Their shambling gait played at the mechanics of a run, but their frail, hobbled bodies could achieve no such speed. Slouched and slumping they gave their chase, no anger or urgency on their wasted faces, only dim resignation to an inexorable duty and an inexorable death.

As Gabriel reached the gap in the wall at the town's edge, two figures emerged to block him. Their weapons were too close to the knight for him to try to talk them out of their decision, so he drew his sword and split both of them open.

One of the fallen was a boy, looking no more than fourteen. He lay in the dirt staring at the sky, clutching at his organs and whimpering while his blue eyes scanned back and forth as though looking for something. Gabriel cursed under his breath. The boy's guts hung out of his body like a squashed beetle's. There here was no saving him.

Gabriel stood over him. In some ways, the boy reminded the knight of himself at that age, with his black hair and dark green eyes. It was purely a similarity of appearance, of course, yet he could not stop his heart from calling back to the young peasant boy that he once had been. "Why did you make me do this?"

The boy wheezed. His mouth moved as though he was trying to speak, but there was not enough air in him. He managed to wheeze, "So that the world," but could not finish the mantra.

Gabriel shook his head, crouched low, and looked him in the eyes. "If your heart has been pure, boy, then Dunrabian will welcome you into his hall. You will know no suffering there." He picked up the boy's weapon, a sharpened antler, from where it had fallen. He held his hand over the kid's eyes, and stabbed him quickly, cleanly through the heart.

Vision distorted by a film of tears, Gabriel looked up to see the Milanites closing on him. He turned and hurried down the path leading between narrow sandstone walls. The tears threatened to overtake him and it took all of his will to hold them back. The trail of dead was growing behind him, and he was beginning to feel like some monstrous destroyer risen from the underworld. As a child, he had pictured nothing but glory and wonder in the realization of his divine mission. The truth was turning out to be a much darker color than the one he had one imagined, and was spattered on all sides with blood.

At the end of the path, the valley walls opened into a vast boulder field. A plateau stood less than a mile in the distance, a crude staircase carved into its side. Gabriel climbed atop one of the stones and leapt from perch to perch. Scorpions emerged from small black holes bored into the boulders. At first, they seemed to be merely a part of the natural order of the place. But, as the poisonous insects shot forth from their burrows, tails poised to sting, it became clear that something else was at work. They appeared only from the boulders that Gabriel stepped on, directed there by the island's malevolent force.

He managed to avoid the scorpions until the final boulder. Preparing to make the leap from the rock to the staircase in the side of the plateau, his exhausted legs buckled under him and he fell. As he did, one of the insects stung him in the calf. He hissed in pain, crushed the insect beneath his fist, and fell over the side of the rock, landing heavily on the ground.

Head swimming with dehydration, hunger, and the poison now seeping into his bloodstream, Gabriel made his way up the stairs. His talents enabled him to ignore pain, but could no longer force his exhausted body to run. His legs quivered beneath him as he reached the top of the plateau. When he looked back, he saw the Milanites gaining on him, some close enough that he could see the ghostly hunger in their eyes.

In accordance with the unnatural geographic laws of the island, the plateau's surface was an entirely different landscape than any of those the knight had previously encountered on the island. It might as well have been another planet. The flat ground was cracked and broken by the sun. Not a piece of vegetation grew anywhere in sight. Waves of heat radiated off the blasted expanse. Far in the distance stood the wavering image of a spindly black tower rising out of the center of the plateau and stabbing at the sky like an angry finger.

"The Spire," Gabriel whispered in awe.

His knees buckled under him as a wave of emotion coursed through his body. After a lifetime of obsessing over the legend of the battle against Elezear, he'd finally reached the very place where those ancient events occurred. He finally stood upon the ground where, five hundred years before, the great army fought the demon. It was the same place where Milan, the first Holy Knight, gave up his immortal soul so that the world may live. *And it is here*, Gabriel thought, *that my destiny will be realized.*

He looked back once more to see the Milanites nearing the top of the staircase. He wondered if they would survive the long march across the sunbaked expanse, and guessed that they would not. They were a pitiful group, yet he could not help but marvel at their devotion, no matter how insane its cause. In a way, he realized, they were more like him than any of the people he'd ever met in the Church. They lived for nothing but their duty, and he admired them for it.

The knight renewed his vow to return for the Milanites after he destroyed Elezear. He'd cross back over the Tempest Gate himself, if he had to, and then they would know that he truly was the prophesied Holy Knight, just as the entire world would know. A wave of euphoria surged through him. He was so close to the culminating act of his knighthood, the one that would ensure the glory of his memory forever, that it no longer seemed to matter that he had not eaten or slept in days. When he started towards the Spire, his leg already swollen and burned from the scorpion's venom, he did so with a smile.

The Tempest Gate swirled on the horizon beyond the demon's tower. As he got closer, Gabriel was struck with the strange sensation that he was closing in on the Gate much faster than he was closing in on the Spire. Stopping to examine this perceptual oddity, he realized he wasn't closing in on the storm—it was closing in on him. The entire wall was collapsing in on the center of the island.

He staggered towards the Spire as quickly as his battered body would allow, but the maelstrom reached the plateau in seconds. Walls of rain advanced with a deafening roar, first swallowing up the Spire and then blasting Gabriel over and sending him skidding across the ground. Visibility was less than a few feet in any direction when he staggered to his feet. He no longer had any idea where the demon's tower stood. He could only guess at some random course to head in and pray that it was the right one.

The knight weaved blindly through the mud for a long time before he encountered the first Milanite. Dressed in an ill-fitting coat of chainmail, the emaciated man lurched expressionlessly at him with a corroded sword. Gabriel ducked the blade and slashed the man's belly open where it was exposed just below his armor. The Milanite fell indifferently to the ground and died without a sound.

Gabriel looked about. More silhouettes staggered through the mist all around him. He crouched low in the fog and watched. They were fanned out searching for him, the entire procession seeming to move on an identical course.

Though they appeared to be as storm-blinded as he, they moved with a deliberate certainty. The knight guessed that their path took them to the Spire, the place that they were sworn to protect. Perhaps they maneuvered by some instinctive sense of direction, one obtained from their unholy relationship with the place. Or so Gabriel hoped, because without some kind of lead to follow, he could wander around in that storm forever and never find the demon. Gauging the direction the Milanites headed in, he bit down against the pain and staggered forward.

Several times he collided with his hunters. They appeared in the downpour before him, too suddenly for him to change his course. Sometimes he was able to drop them with a nonfatal blow with the handle of his sword. Other times, he was unable to spare their lives. As the strange journey seemed to go on for miles, Gabriel wondered if he would have to wade through every one of them before he would make it to the foot of the demon's tower. It was beginning to seem as though he would have to climb over their backs to reach Elezear's doorstep.

The cluster of Milanites eventually thinned out, and then disappeared completely. Gabriel looked over his shoulder for his pursuers, saw none, and turned back around just before colliding with the black wall of the Spire looming out of the mist before him. He skidded to a halt, bracing himself against the cold, slick stone.

The knight circled around the base of the tower until he found a staircase. The stairs were narrow, barely more than two feet wide, and slick with rain. Moving slowly to keep from falling, he had made it maybe a hundred feet when a woman lunged out of the murk before him, clutching at his eyes with her bare, bony fingers. Gabriel pivoted towards the wall so that she slicked off of his body and went plummeting over the Spire's side. She looked straight at him as she disappeared into the darkness to her death. Her blank expression did not change in the slightest.

The rain and hail grew fiercer as he climbed, until his back bowed under the force. He lumbered on with plodding steps, bracing himself against the wall to stay upright. Even after the deluge forced him to his knees, he crawled over the stairs on all fours, roaring at the storm overhead, "You'll have to pulverize every bone in my body before you can stop me."

It seemed as though the storm was willing and able to comply with his demand. It hammered down on him furiously, flattening him out on the ground and forcing him to drag himself along the stairs on his stomach. But it did not break him, and he continued on in his crawling manner until he reached the end of the stairs and the mouth of the cave just beyond them.

The knight lay on the dry floor of that dark space, gathering himself while the rain echoed like war drums inside. His breath came out in smoky tufts in the frigid air, but it was not the cold that set every hair of his body on end like a dog's hackles – it was the malevolent presence that he sensed lurking in the darkness.

He untied the makeshift sack from his waist and laid the torch and the flint out on the floor. Though soaked with water, it still smelled of the fuel it had been soaked in. He struck the flint to light it. Sparks leapt and died on the cloth several times before one finally caught. A tiny wisp of smoke curled into the air. Gabriel dropped the flint and knelt over this little hope with his hands cupped around it. He blew gently over the area until the flame took. Even then it was a sputtering, meager light that he bore into the immense darkness.

He made it only a few feet more into the cavernous space when a voice spoke. "You're early."

Gabriel stopped. The words had been human, but not the voice. Instead, it had sounded like some nightmarish multitude of sounds, as though a cacophony of hysterical screams and baying dogs and moaning arctic winds had been combined together and shaped into syllables. The sound of it sent a shiver through the knight, and he nearly cried out in terror. Nearly, but not quite.

Gabriel remembered his title and the purpose he had been born for. He was the Holy Knight, and had no cause to fear anyone or anything. When he spoke, he did so without the slightest tremor. "Wrong, Elezear. I am right on time."

"My last meal was brought only weeks ago."

"You should be thankful to have eaten so recently, for that meal will be your last." Gabriel stepped deeper into the cave, waving his torch about to locate the demon. "I am not one of your sniveling caretakers."

The chamber was quiet for some time before the voice spoke again. "You are no Milanite."

"No," Gabriel laughed. "I am definitely not of their ilk."

"You are a messenger of fools, then, which is always a fool himself."

"I am no messenger, and no fool. I am the Holy Knight of the Church of Dunrabian."

"A knight of the court of fools is a fool just the same," the demon said. A terrible shriek filled the cave, a maddening sound that must have been laughter. "Come then, messenger, and tell me what news you bring."

"I bring no news for you." Gabriel wheeled about with his flame, searching in vain for his enemy.

"You bring much news. Yes, you bring news that humanity has chosen to break its pact with me. You bring news that your race needs to be reminded of darkness. You bring news that the time has come for Elezear to return to the world."

Gabriel reached the far wall of the cave. He'd traversed the breadth of the floor and found nothing. "Funny, for I am unaware of such a message."

"It is always that way. A fool's message comes in what he fails to say. That is the nature of fools, and their messages."

Gabriel walked the length of the wall with his sword at the ready, several times startling and nearly striking at shadows. "I tell you again, I am no fool."

"No fool ever believes he is so. That's why he is a fool. But you come from the court of fools, so there is no other thing for you to be. Now, fool, I will offer you the same deal I offered your predecessor. Offer up your soul, and I will spare your race. Do it not, and I will turn all that you know to ash."

Gabriel waved his torch overhead to look for the demon above him, but the meager light could not penetrate the dark heights. "I have not come to feed you. I have come to destroy you."

"I say again, and one last time, give yourself up, or bear the burden of your race's ruin. You have broken the pact, and for that you must pay penance. Such is the law."

"The only law I follow is the law written in the Book."

"The law that I am was written long before. It was built into the foundations of this universe before time began, and it will be written there still at the end of time, long after the last copy of your Book is turned to dust and blown away. Now, will you pay penance for your folly, fool?"

Gabriel slashed his sword into the darkness in frustration. "I have not come to pay, but to collect."

"So, your decision is made?"

"It is. Now show yourself."

"But I already have."

The darkness closed in around Gabriel, a physical force that knocked the torch from his hand. It coiled around his body, lifted him up into the air, and stretched his arms out painfully to his sides.

Gabriel strained with all his power to break his sword arm free, but he was powerless against the force that bound him. "You're a coward," the knight spat. "You wield your sorcery from the darkness, instead of facing me."

Elezear laughed. "You still don't understand, little knight. I don't hide in the darkness. I *am* the darkness."

Black vapors entered Gabriel's nostrils. He could feel the malignant things churning coldly within him, and experienced the horrific sensation of a foreign entity breathing within his own lungs.

"Perhaps you would prefer a more recognizable form," Elezear said.

The torch burning on the floor flared up and created a broad halo of light. From the darkness beyond the illumination, a massive form slithered into view. It was a three-headed serpent, rearing up into the air, hissing and snapping its jaws as poison dripped from its fangs and landed sizzling on the cave floor. Gabriel recognized the form as Stain, nemesis of Dunrabian, the demon impaled upon the Unicorn's horn in the Church's symbol.

"Or, perhaps a different form is called for, to suit the dragon-slayer?"

The snake transformed into an enormous wyrm looming up into the vaulted cave, neck stretched forward so that it looked into Gabriel's face. Its eye sockets were black, but rather than simple shadow, the darkness swarmed with horrific life.

"But no, of course not," Elezear said. "For the great knight, only a more familiar face will suffice."

The dragon disappeared and the cave fell into silence. Moments later, a human figure strode out of the shadows into the torchlight. It took Gabriel a moment to realize that the person he was looking at was a replica of himself, identical in every way, except for the black eyes. "Now do you recognize the face of your destruction?"

Gabriel screamed in horror at the sight of the demon mimicking his own body. "Dunrabian," he cried out, "help me."

Elezear laughed. "He will not answer. I am closer to your god than you will ever be. You mistake your hubris for heroism, little knight, and you have overstepped your boundaries. In doing so, you've brought ruin upon your world." It cocked its head aside and smirked, studying him. "Tell me, how does that knowledge feel?"

Gabriel strained so hard to escape that the muscles in his shoulders tore. Despite his efforts, he did not move an inch. The coiling, vaporous darkness stirred within him again, this time constricting his heart. Against his will, he cried out in pain. "Dunrabian, this is not the destiny I was supposed to have."

Elezear looked deep into Gabriel's eyes, as though examining something within them. The dark tendrils stretched the knight's arms to the point of tearing, and clutched his heart in a brutal gasp.

"The world will pay for your arrogance. For centuries, the Milanites have purchased peace for your race, but their sacrifice cannot pay the price of your transgression. One from your world will have to do that, but experience has taught me that your people require hard, hard lessons before they are able to learn. Whether or not they will survive the coming lesson long enough to learn from it, remains to be seen."

Gabriel slipped in and out of consciousness. His life drifted away from him. The muscles and sinew in his arms snapped. Just before his vision faded completely, and death's cold hands embraced him, he managed to wheeze a single utterance. "Take my soul," he said.

Elezear ceased its attack. It leaned closer, as if to see deeper into his eyes. "I wondered if you would," it said. "It's a fate worse than death, you know. Even in the underworld, there is hope for redemption, but if you give your soul to me, it will be mine forever."

"Spare me your melodrama," Gabriel choked. "I will give you my soul, so that the world may live." He sneered. "But know this, demon: I am Gabriel, Holy Knight, and Arm of the Sword of Dunrabian. I may not be able to defeat you, but I will battle you every moment we spend together in eternity."

Elezear stepped back, seemingly oblivious to Gabriel's bravado. Its face twisted in unnatural hunger, black eyes stirring like storm clouds. "Do you give your soul to me? You must say the words."

Gabriel let out a ragged breath. He forced himself to be steady so that his voice would not tremble when he spoke. "I give my soul to you," he said.

Pain exploded in his chest. His body went into spasms. The end was coming, but instead of fear, he felt only a wave of renewed determination run through him. His failed showdown with Elezear was all part of his destiny. It was, in fact, the culminating test of his faith. It had to be, for he was the Holy Knight, and Dunrabian's chosen Arm could not fall so easily. His soul would go into the final dark not as a sacrifice, but as a conqueror. Gabriel looked into his nemesis' black eyes. "The end of my flesh is only the beginning of our battle," he said.

For a moment, the demon relented in its attack, as though considering what the knight had said. It was a brief respite, but long enough for Gabriel to force a smile onto his lips. Elezear roared and commenced its assault.

Gabriel nearly cried out at the pain, but retained his stoic composure. He would not leave the world mewling like a frightened child. He stared steadily into the demon's eyes, and laughed. "All light," he said, "is forged in war with darkness." Just as his heart ruptured, and the world before his eyes turned black, Gabriel was certain that Elezear shuddered before him.

www.ingramcontent.com/pod-product-compliance
Lightning Source LLC
Chambersburg PA
CBHW070808120626
46557CB00002B/756